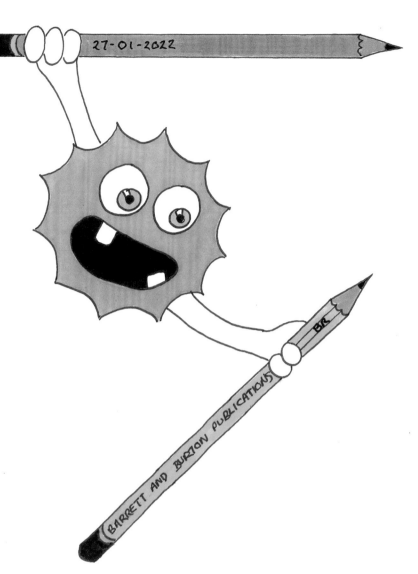

27-01-2022

For Charlotte, Sophie,
Daisy & Skylar

For letting us read you hours
upon hours of bedtime stories

BORIS THE GERM

Written by Gavin Barrett
Illustrated by Martin Burton

Millions and billions
and trillions of germs.

They do what they want,
purely on their own terms.

They're so very tiny,
they go where they like.

Undercover they lurk,
always waiting to strike.

So who are these tiny invisible friends?
Let's take a quick look with a microscope lens.
There's one already, now try not to squirm.
This ones called Boris. Boris the germ!

But what does he do when he's not sitting still?
I'll tell you, he's looking to make someone ill.
See he might look quite cute with his wide smirking grin,

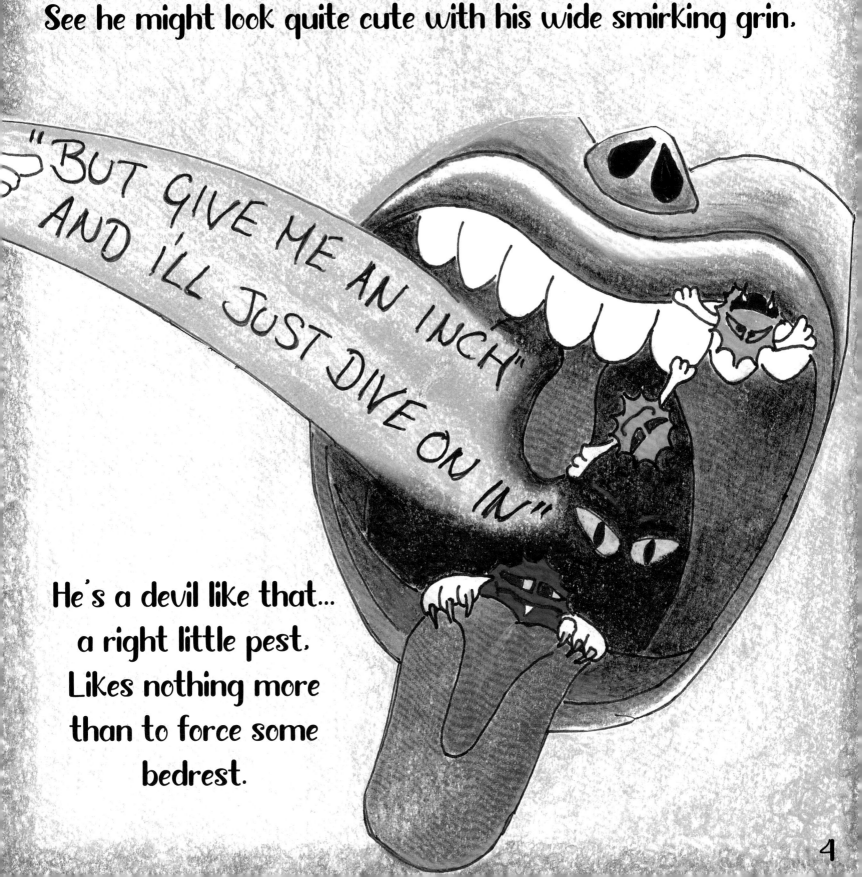

"BUT GIVE ME AN INCH" AND I'LL JUST DIVE ON IN"

He's a devil like that...
a right little pest.
Likes nothing more
than to force some
bedrest.

Now why does he do this? He might not know why.
But his friends do it and they're in no short supply.
Cos Boris can make some more friends on his own.
Soon there's two and then four and the team has now grown.
Eight and then sixteen, anything goes.
Safety in numbers, as the party then grows.

But Boris and friends are not welcome round here. Leave them unchecked and they won't disappear.

If you want to avoid feeling rough with a cold.
We need to teach germs to just
do as they're told.

This party's no fun for us humans you see,
Cos while Boris and friends dance around, it is he,
Who is having the fun at the humans expense,
We need to fight back, time to launch a defence,
But what do we use so we keep them at bay?

Catapult?

Arrows?

Thankfully, all of us have what we need.
Some soap and some water, Boris take heed!

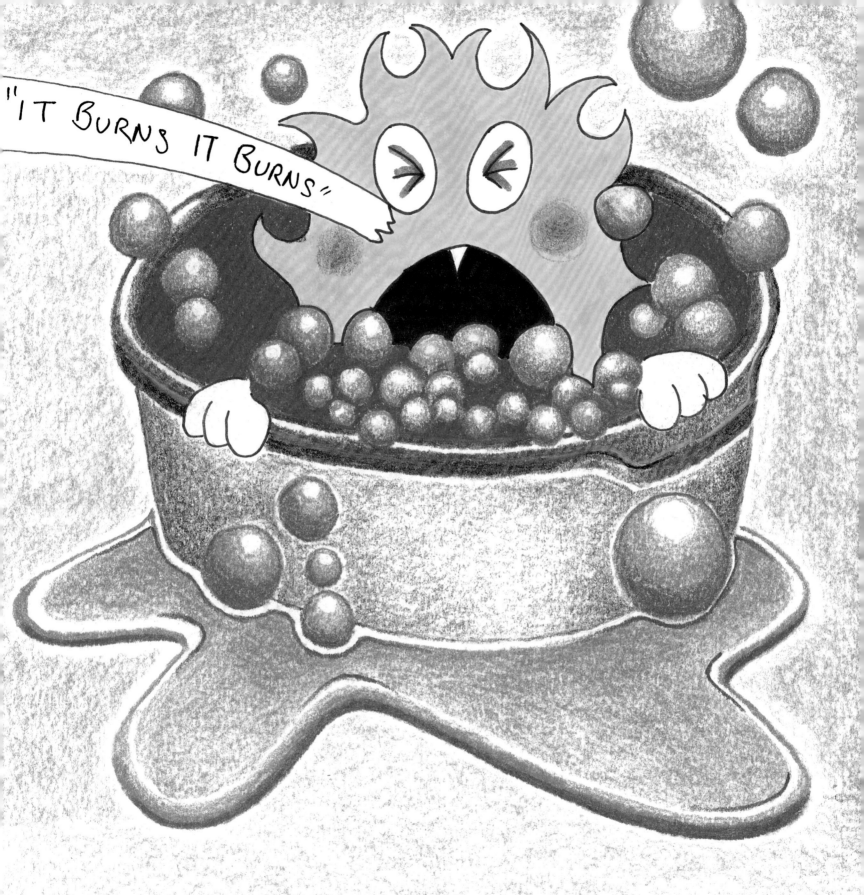

He runs right away,
From this magical liquid "I don't want to play"

Boris and friends take a trip down the sink,
"PARTY DOWN THERE WITH SOME CRISPS AND A DRINK!
Let's live our lives in a separate place.
You have some fun, but give us lot some space."

We can't do the things we enjoy when we're sick,
Like seeing our friends, and the hobbies we pick.

I wish you well Boris, but it's time that you went.
Some time on your own will be time that's well spent.

This multiply game might be good fun for you,
But we've all had enough: you and me, we are through.

So remember young folks,
keep an eye on the prize,
keep your hands clean,
cut those germs down to size.

Soap is the key, it's what
Boris won't stand.
Water alone, he'll just stay
on your hand.

It might be a small thing,
but it's valuable time.
If it helps, perhaps think of
this short little rhyme.